ZAPATO POWER
FREDDIE RAMOS SPRINGS INTO ACTION

JACQUELINE JULES   art by MIGUEL BENÍTEZ

Albert Whitman & Company
Chicago, Illinois

Don't miss the first **Zapato Power** book!

ZAPATO POWER
FREDDIE RAMOS TAKES OFF

by Jacqueline Jules
illustrated by Miguel Benítez

Library of Congress Cataloging-in-Publication Data
Jules, Jacqueline, 1956-
Zapato power : Freddie Ramos springs into action! / by Jacqueline Jules ;
illustrated by Miguel Benítez.
p. cm.
Summary: When a very important inventor needs rescuing,
Freddie Ramos activates his special sneakers and becomes a superhero.
ISBN 978-0-8075-9481-0
[1. Superheroes—Fiction. 2. Inventions—Fiction. 3. Sneakers—Fiction.
4. Hispanic Americans—Fiction.] I. Benítez, Miguel, ill.
II. Title. III. Title: Freddie Ramos springs into action!
PZ7.J92947Zan 2010   [Fic]—dc22   2010002769

10 9 8 7 6 5 4 3 2 1 LB 15 14 13 12 11 10

For more information about Albert Whitman & Company,
visit our web site at www.albertwhitman.com

For my students. —JJ
For Dee & Nat. —MB

CONTENTS

1. A Thump in the Morning

THUMP-BUMP! THUMP-BUMP! THUMP-BUMP!

I sat up in bed and rubbed my eyes.

THUMP-BUMP! THUMP-BUMP! THUMP-BUMP!

Who was making noise so early on a Sunday morning? And right outside my window?

CRaSH! WaaaaaaaGH!

It sounded like broken glass. And somebody crying!

I grabbed my purple sneakers. There was no time to get dressed. Somebody at Starwood Park needed help—maybe even a hero's help. And with my purple sneakers, I had Zapato Power! That's super speed, the kind superheroes have.

ZOOM! ZOOM! ZaPaTO!

I ran outside in my red and blue pajamas. My purple sneakers were smoking. I was ready to help.

"WaaaaaGH!"
"Ruff! Ruff!"

Gio, my next-door neighbor, cried while his little dog, Puppy, barked at a big hole in Mrs. Tran's window.

"Did you break that window?" I asked Gio.

"My ball broke it when I bounced it on the wall."

Puppy agreed. "Ruff! Ruff!"

Gio is five. He only goes to kindergarten in the morning. He hasn't had time to learn a lot of things—like how neighbors don't like basketballs crashing into their apartments.

"Watch out!" I shouted.

Mrs. Tran hollered something in a language we didn't understand and threw Gio's basketball out of the hole in her window.

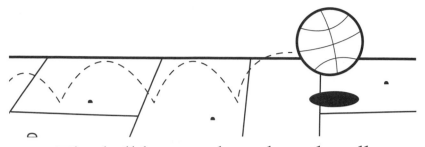

The ball bounced on the sidewalk and rolled down the hill to the street.

"My ball!" Gio cried.

He chased after it, but the basketball was way too fast for him. And a red car was coming around the corner. If Gio wasn't smart enough not to bounce a basketball off a window, he might not be smart enough to stay out of the street. It was time to use my super speed to save the day.

ZOOM! ZOOM! ZAPATO!

In one blink, I was at the curb, scooping up the ball, just as the red car sped by.

"You saved my ball!" Gio said, as he rushed up to me. "You're fast!"

I sure was. With my purple zapatos, I could save a ball from going into the street. I could save a puppy from a speeding car. I could even outrun a train. But I couldn't save Gio from Mrs. Tran, his mother, and his sister, Maria.

"What were you thinking?" Gio's mom came down the hill with Puppy at her heels. "Why were you throwing a ball against the building?"

"Who's going to fix my window?" Mrs. Tran asked.

"You're in trouble now," Maria said.

"I'm sorry!" Gio cried. "Lo siento."

"Ruff! Ruff!" Puppy said.

Everybody was barking, crying, or asking questions. I used my Zapato Power to get out of there, fast.

ZOOM! ZOOM! ZAPATO!

In half a blink, I was at Mr. Vaslov's toolshed. He takes care of Starwood Park. If something's broken, Mr. Vaslov is the guy to fix it.

I knocked on the door.

"Freddie!" Mr. Vaslov said, when he saw me. "What are you doing in your pajamas?"

I looked down at my blue and red striped pajama pants. "Superheroes don't always have time to get dressed," I said.

Mr. Vaslov smiled and waved me inside his toolshed with a screwdriver. I looked around at all the tools and cut-up computers. Mr. Vaslov does more than take care of Starwood Park. He invents things like special shoes that go ninety miles an hour. I have Zapato Power because of Mr. Vaslov.

"So what's the problem?" Mr. Vaslov asked.

I told him about Gio and Mrs. Tran's window. He picked up a broom and started out the door.

"Time for some clean-up," he said.

"Do you need help?" I asked.

Mr. Vaslov pushed back his bushy gray hair. "Sounds like everybody is pretty upset. I'd stay out of the way for a while if I were you."

Just then, we heard the metro train rumble on its overhead track in the back of the building. My feet started to tingle in my sneakers. I waved at Mr. Vaslov. Then I took off…

ZOOM! ZOOM! ZAPATO!

2. A Softer Ball

The metro train goes right by
Starwood Park. I've been racing
it since I moved here, just for fun.
But when Mr. Vaslov gave me my
purple zapatos, it got a lot more
interesting.

I ran beside the overhead track.
Smoke swirled around me as my
legs spun faster and faster. The wind

whooshed against
my face so hard, I
had to blink my
eyes. Rápido!
I zipped past
the train, flying
on the ground.
ZAPATO
POWER! Nothing
could touch me! I was
faster than a rocket!
But still too young to leave the
house without telling my mother.

"FREDDIE! WHERE ARE YOU?" Mom shouted all over Starwood Park.

 ZOOM! ZOOM! ZAPATO!

I raced back up the hill to where Mom stood with her hands on her hips. "Where did you go? I was worried."

"To tell Mr. Vaslov about Mrs. Tran's window," I said.

"I'm glad you're all right."

Mom hugged me. She's been mushy ever since last year, when we lost my soldier dad and my grandmother, Abuela. Mom says we only have each other now, so she deserves extra hugs whenever she gets worried about me.

"And I'm glad you know better than to throw balls through windows," Mom added.

"Gio needs a softer ball," I said.

"Yes, he does," a deep voice behind us agreed. It was Mr. Vaslov. He held a blue and white beach ball.

Mom laughed. "Gio won't break any windows with that!"

"I know." Mr. Vaslov smiled. "That's why I'm giving it to him."

"You're such a nice man!" Mom

said. "We're lucky to have you at Starwood Park."

Mom was right about Mr. Vaslov. He gave me my purple zapatos, and he gave Gio a new ball without yelling at him for breaking the window.

"Accidents happen," Mr. Vaslov said. "It's part of life."

"Thanks!" Gio shouted, as he took the beach ball. "Can I play with it now?"

"Throw it as high as you want," Mr. Vaslov said. "It shouldn't hurt anything!"

We all stood watching Gio toss the ball for a few minutes. Then Mom put her hand on my shoulder.

"Freddie? Do you know you're still wearing pajamas?"

3. An On-Off Switch

The rest of my Sunday wasn't too exciting. We didn't have anything to do except clean the house. I really miss my abuela on Sundays. When she was alive, we went over to her house for dinner. Now, Mom and I usually clean Claude the Second's cage. Cleaning guinea pig poop is just

not as much fun as eating tamales.
And Mom gets cranky when
Claude the Second waddles off his
newspaper and leaves tiny presents
on the carpet.

"Get the vacuum cleaner!" Mom
ordered, scooping up my guinea pig.

I rushed down the hall, forgetting all about the smoke that comes out of my purple zapatos every time I run.

"Thanks!" Mom said, handing me Claude the Second so she could take the vacuum. "You were so fast you were smoking!"

Luckily, Mom cared more about cleaning up Claude the Second's poop than why I could run so fast. She didn't know about my Zapato Power. Mom already worried enough. Knowing I had super speed and was trying to be a superhero wouldn't make her feel any better. I needed to be more careful. My purple zapatos were just fine when I walked. But the second I picked up some speed, I zoomed off like a rocket! It wasn't just a problem in front of my mom, it was a problem on the playground.

"How come you turn into a puff of smoke when you run?" my friend Maria asked the next day at recess.

Super speed is not an easy thing to hide during a basketball game.

"Come on, Freddie!" Hamza said. "Don't be a hog. Let somebody else get some points for a change."

"How do you know it's Freddie?" Maria asked. "All I can see is a magic wind stealing the ball."

I tried to slow down, but my super zapatos wouldn't let me. And my hands were just as itchy as my feet.

With super speed, I was always next to the ball. It was natural to grab it and go for the hoop. That's what a basketball player does.

"I quit!" Geraldo shouted, when I got my thirtieth point. "The rest of us don't have a chance!"

P.E. wasn't any better than recess that day. Mr. Gooley, our gym teacher, took us outside to practice the fifty-yard dash.

"Freddie!" Mr. Gooley hollered. "You can't run across the field before I blow the whistle. It's not fair."

Zapato Power was the best thing on earth when I was alone. But when I was with my friends, it felt a little like cheating.

"What's wrong, Freddie?" Mr. Vaslov asked me after school on Monday. "You've lost your superhero smile."

We sat down on the steps of

his toolshed. Mr. Vaslov listened carefully as I explained the problem.

"Your shoes need an on-off switch." Mr. Vaslov patted my shoulder.

"That's a great idea!"

Mr. Vaslov stroked his chin, thinking. "Now's the time to add improvements, while I'm still developing and testing the shoes."

"And trying to make a second pair," I added.

"Right again, Freddie." Mr. Vaslov chuckled. "I still haven't figured out how to make my invention work for anybody but you."

"But what about controls? Do you think you can make them?" I asked.

Mr. Vaslov leaned down and touched the silver wings on the sides of my shoes. His face looked like my mom's when she's trying to decide if she can buy new clothes for me.

"Give me a few days to come up with something, Freddie. I'll do the best I can."

4. Inventions Take Time

I'm not the most patient guy.
Every afternoon, I knocked on Mr.
Vaslov's toolshed. He opened the
door halfway to talk to me.

"Are you finished?"

"Not yet," Mr. Vaslov answered.
"But I have a great idea."

"What?" I asked.

"A wristband with a button you can press."

"Sounds great! When will it be ready?"

"Inventions take time, Freddie." Mr. Vaslov gently closed the door.

The days went by slowly. I got tired of watching my friends play basketball at recess while I pretended to have a sore ankle. And Mr. Gooley got tired of my excuses about why I couldn't run during P.E.

"What hurts today, Freddie?" Mr. Gooley asked, when I came up to him, holding my hand over my left ear.

Mr. Gooley let me sit on the bench again, but I could tell he was getting suspicious. I didn't have any body parts left to  complain about. Keeping my super speed a secret was taking a lot of brainwork. It's not easy to come up with good excuses.

"Mr. Vaslov!" I knocked on the toolshed door a week later. "Is my on-off switch working yet?"

For the first time, no one answered. I knocked again, louder and harder. The door pushed open. I saw a bunch of wires and a purple wristband on the table. Was that the wristband Mr. Vaslov was making for me?

I stood outside the toolshed for a few minutes, debating if I should go inside when Mr. Vaslov wasn't there. Then, I heard crying.

"**WaaaaaGH!**"

Who was in trouble? From the moment I got my purple zapatos, I'd been watching out for chances to be a hero. Once, I saved Gio's puppy from a speeding car. I saved his basketball, too, after Mrs. Tran threw it out the window. But being a superhero meant helping people all the time.

"**WaaaaaGH!**" The sound was behind me, way up near my apartment, 29G.

I couldn't resist. I turned around.

ZOOM! ZOOM! ZaPaTO!

In half a blink, I was standing in front of Gio. His crying was a lot louder and slobbery in person than it was from far away.

"My ball," he wailed, "the one Mr. Vaslov gave me. It's gone!"

This wasn't exactly a superhero rescue. But Gio was my friend and my neighbor. I zipped around the building in my purple zapatos, to see if I could find his ball. No luck.

"Where did you see it last?" I asked.

"When I was playing with it," he answered.

Talking to Gio made me feel like a detective. I had to ask a lot of questions to get any information. "Where were you playing with it?"

He pointed to the grass behind

Building G. "Mr. Vaslov told me to throw the ball up in the air, not at the windows or the wall."

"Good advice," I said.

ZOOM! ZOOM! ZAPATO!

I ran around the building a couple more times, but I still couldn't find Gio's ball. He went inside to get Puppy and I decided to try to find Mr. Vaslov again. Maybe he knew what had happened to Gio's ball. Nobody knew what was going on at Starwood Park like Mr. Vaslov.

When I got back to the toolshed, the door was still open. Mr. Vaslov wasn't anywhere around. I saw the purple wristband on the table again. Was it ready yet?

I stepped inside the toolshed for a closer look.

5. The Purple Wristband

The purple wristband had a
flashing white light in the middle of
a clear button. My on-off switch! I
couldn't wait to try it. But where was
Mr. Vaslov?

It didn't feel quite right to be
snooping around his toolshed, the
place where he invented my super

shoes. But Mr. Vaslov's toolshed didn't seem quite right, either. Stuff was blinking, beeping, and talking. Two computers had little white letters running across the screen. Some kind of radio made noise every couple of seconds. And a little TV set on a top shelf was playing a news show. My mom always makes me turn everything off before I leave 29G unless we're planning to come

right back. She also makes me eat my food before I leave the house. There was an uneaten peanut butter sandwich with a glass of milk on the table. Mr. Vaslov had to be coming back soon.

About ten minutes went by, but Mr. Vaslov still didn't show up. It was hard to stay and it was hard to leave. What about the purple wristband? Could I try it on?

If Mr. Vaslov didn't yell at Gio for breaking Mrs. Tran's window, he probably wouldn't yell at me for trying on the wristband. After all, he was making it for me. I looked through the doorway one more time to make sure he wasn't coming. Then, I picked up the wristband.

I put it on my right arm. It was just the right size. And I loved the little  flashing light. It looked like a radio bracelet a spaceman might wear.

Why didn't Mr. Vaslov come back? Should I try to find him?

I left the toolshed, still wearing the purple wristband. It was just too great to take off my arm. My eyes stayed on the flashing light beneath the clear button. What would happen if I pressed it?

It hummed under my finger. Then I felt a tingling in my feet, just like when my purple zapatos are itching for a rocket race. But something was different about it. What? The second I moved, I figured out why.

BOING! I wasn't running. **BOING!** I was jumping! The wristband gave me a new power. **BOING!** I shot up into the air, floated for a second or two, and then came down. It was almost like flying. **BOING! BOING! BOING!**

I jumped over the green dumpster for recycling. **BOING! BOING! BOING!** Each time I hit the ground, white smoke gushed out of my heels.

How high could I go? **BOING! BOING! BOING!** I jumped beside a big oak tree and reached for a big fat branch. It was easy to take hold and climb right in.

The branches above me were like a ladder. I decided to climb higher to see if I could find Mr. Vaslov from above. In no time, I was way above the ground, able to see all over Starwood Park.

Mr. Vaslov wasn't watering flowers

near the front entrance sign or
sweeping up any of the sidewalks.
I didn't see him coming out of any
of the apartment doors, either.

But I did see Gio's blue and
white beach ball. It bounced off the
roof of a new building on the edge
of Starwood Park. That building
was just finished and didn't have
people moved in yet. What was
Gio's ball doing way over there?

6. Are You Stuck?

As I watched Gio's ball bounce off the roof of the new building and fall to the ground, my tree shook in the wind. It jiggled my brain and I figured something out. The wind must have taken Gio's beach ball! They get blown around, just like kites.

I had solved the mystery of Gio's

missing ball. But I had another problem. How was I going to get down from the tree? The green ground straight below me looked so far away and so hard. I squeezed the trunk tighter and tighter.

My body felt like someone had poured glue all over it. I learned something new. It is easier to climb up a tree than down it.

The sun dropped lower in the sky. Mom would come home from work soon. When she didn't see me at the table, doing my homework, she would start calling my name all over Starwood Park. The whole

neighborhood
would hear her
hollering when
she found me clinging
to a tree with both
arms and legs. This
was not my day to be a
brave superhero.

"WHAT ARE YOU
DOING UP THERE?"
Gio called. Gio found me before my
mother did. It didn't cheer me up.
Gio was in kindergarten! What if
he told his friends about this?

"Ruff! Ruff!" Puppy was with
him. The dog wanted to know why

I was in the tree, too.

Gio and Puppy looked so small way down below at the bottom. Now I knew why cats got stuck in trees. Would they have to call the fire department for me? Would I be on the TV news?

"WHAT ARE YOU DOING UP THERE?" Gio repeated.

I had to come up with something fast—a reason that would make me sound smart instead of like a meowing cat.

"LOOKING FOR
MR. VASLOV! HAVE
YOU SEEN HIM?"
I shouted.

Gio shook his
head. Puppy barked.
"Ruff! Ruff!"

Where was Mr. Vaslov? He had
a ladder. I'd seen him use it lots of
times. I wished he was around to help
me down.

"ARE YOU STUCK?" Gio called
up.

How could I tell the truth? What

kind of superhero gets stuck in a tree like a cat?

"I'LL HELP YOU!" Gio said, climbing into the tree.

Puppy barked. "Ruff! Ruff!"

Superheroes shouldn't be rescued by kindergartners! I looked down at Gio, climbing one branch after another. What if he got scared when he got this high up, too? Then we'd both be crying like cats in the tree. I had no choice. I moved my foot down a little and found the branch below me. The tree was just like a ladder. I could go down the same way I went up—

one branch at a time.

"Come on!" Gio stopped climbing and started cheering for me. "You can do it, Freddie. I know you can."

And I did, just in time for my mother to start calling.

"FREDDIE! WHERE ARE YOU? IT'S TIME FOR DINNER!"

Gio grabbed my hand and we walked back to 29G with Puppy at our heels. "Ruff! Ruff!"

For dinner, Mom and I had tamales—the microwave kind.

"Sorry, Freddie," Mom apologized. "There's no time after work to cook like Abuela did."

"Her tamales were good," I agreed. "But these are just fine."

"No, no." Mom shook her head, wiggling her gold hoop earrings. "No box is as good as Abuela's cooking."

On Sundays, Abuela made all my favorites like pupusas stuffed with cheese, refried beans, and yucca. I miss arroz con leche—rice pudding—the most, because the kind that comes in plastic cups doesn't taste as good.

Abuela died six months after my soldier dad. It was really hard to have two funerals in one year. That was before we moved to Starwood Park. Before my mom learned how to smile again.

"How about a popsicle for dessert?" Mom asked, getting up from the table. On weeknights, all our food comes from the freezer or the delivery man.

"Sure!" I said. "Do you have red ones?"

We ate our popsicles on the front step. It was a nice night with lots of stars.

"How much homework do you have?" Mom asked.

"Not much." I took another lick of my popsicle.

"How much is not much?" Mom raised her eyebrows. She was serious about school. Her plan was to save all her money and send me to college one day.

Before I could say I only had a few math problems and some social studies reading, Mom's cell phone jingled with music.

"Hola?" She put her finger on the other ear so she could hear better. "Hello? You want to speak to

who? Freddie?"

"Who is it?" I asked, gulping down my last bite of popsicle.

"Mr. Vaslov," Mom said. Her voice sounded puzzled. "He said your name and then the phone went dead."

7. A Superhero with a Mom

"Mr. Vaslov!" I stood up and shouted. "I tried to find him all day!"

"I wonder what he wants," Mom said.

That's when my face heated up. He was calling about the purple wristband! Mr. Vaslov must have been wondering where it was.

I hoped he wasn't angry with me. I shouldn't have taken it without asking. I needed to apologize.

"You look worried, Freddie," Mom said. "Is anything wrong?"

"I'm not sure," I said. "But I'd like to talk to Mr. Vaslov."

"It's still early," Mom said. "Let's go over to his place and see if he's there."

Good idea. I'd always wanted to see inside Mr. Vaslov's apartment. I wondered if he had cut-up computers and tools in there, too.

We walked over to 10B, where Mr. Vaslov lived, and rang the

doorbell three times. No one answered.

"Let's try the toolshed," I said.

The door was half open, just like I'd left it. And the computers were still blinking, the radio still beeping, and the TV still on. But no Mr. Vaslov.

"That's a little strange," Mom said, peeking inside. "He left all the lights on and a glass of milk."

The peanut butter sandwich was still there, too. Why didn't Mr. Vaslov come back to eat his food?

"Where else can we look?" I asked.

"Nowhere," Mom said. "You have

homework and school tomorrow."

"But I need to talk to Mr. Vaslov!"

"In the morning," Mom said, taking my shoulders and turning me around toward 29G.

I was worried about Mr. Vaslov. He had never been missing this long. But superheroes with moms like mine can't go out by themselves after dark. All I could do was set my alarm for six A.M.

As soon as I heard it ring, I jumped out

of bed and put on my super zapatos. Then, I took them off and got dressed. I didn't want to be seen running around in my blue and red pajamas again.

ZOOM! ZOOM! ZAPATO!

I ran over to 10B and rang the doorbell. No answer. I dashed over to the toolshed. The computers were still on and the peanut butter still uneaten.

ZOOM! ZOOM! ZAPATO!

I ran all around Starwood Park.

The only thing I saw was Mr. Vaslov's ladder behind the brand new building, a few feet from Gio's beach ball. Where was Mr. Vaslov?

I ran around the buildings a second time and a third, but the ladder and the ball were still the only things I found. My Zapato Power wasn't working. I needed to use some brain power.

Why was Mr. Vaslov's ladder on the ground? He always picked his stuff up. This was almost as strange as his uneaten peanut butter.

What had I seen Mr. Vaslov use his ladder for? Sometimes he used it to fix stuff on the roof. Is that where he was?

I'd looked everywhere I could for Mr. Vaslov on the ground. The only place left was the air.

I pressed the button on my wristband and shot straight up. **BOING!** Not quite high enough to see the roof. I jumped again. **BOING! BOING! BOING!**

I saw just over the edge. Someone was lying down. He

had bushy gray hair.

"Mr. Vaslov!" I called. "I'm coming!"

BOING! BOING! BOING!

"Freddie!" he called back. "Get the ladder!"

The ladder! **BOING!** I landed on the ground. Why didn't I think of that myself?

My shoes might get me on the roof, but I had no way of getting down. I couldn't help Mr. Vaslov if I got stuck again.

The ladder was big. I got Mom to help me. Together, we leaned it against the gutter and climbed up to Mr. Vaslov. Then Mom called an ambulance. It came right away.

"My ankle hurts," Mr. Vaslov groaned.

"It might be broken," the ambulance man said. "And you have a bump on your head. You have to go to the hospital."

"Who will take care of Starwood Park?" Mr. Vaslov protested, as they put him in the ambulance.

"I will," I promised just before they closed the doors.

"Thanks, Freddie," he said.

When they drove away, Mom put her arms around me. "You saved Mr. Vaslov! You're a superhero!"

Was I? Really?

8. An Extra Button

When Mr. Vaslov came home
from the hospital on crutches,
Starwood Park took care of him just
like he always took care of us.

Mrs. Tran checked on him
every morning to make sure he
was leaning back in his easy chair,
pressing the buttons on the TV

remote, and not running around Starwood Park, trying to fix things. Gio and Maria's mom brought him lunch in the afternoon. And my mom brought him dinner.

"Sorry these burritos are from a micro- wave box," Mom said. "On Sunday, I'll cook you something from scratch."

"No need, Mrs. Ramos," he said.

"I'm a bachelor. I'm used to eating food from the freezer."

We all laughed. Then we got busy eating.

After dinner, we found out why Mr. Vaslov was on the roof.

"I heard Gio crying. Then, I saw his ball blown away by the wind," he began.

"So you went up on the roof to get it for him," I said.

"Yes," Mr. Vaslov continued. "But when I got up there, the ball rolled away from me. I slipped and knocked the ladder down."

"Oh, no!" Mom put her hands on

her cheeks.

"That's why you called me!"
I said.

"Right," Mr. Vaslov said. "We
couldn't talk because my phone
went dead."

"And you were too far away for anyone to hear you yell for help," Mom said.

"Right again," Mr. Vaslov said. "When it got dark, I figured I might as well fall asleep. No one could see me until the morning."

"I'm glad Freddie found you so early," Mom said.

"Me, too." Mr. Vaslov leaned over in his easy chair to pat my shoulder. "Freddie's my hero."

Wow! Both my mom and Mr. Vaslov thought I was a hero. It sure felt better than being stuck in a tree. Was it time to give myself a superhero name? Could I get a special suit that didn't look like my pajamas?

A week later, the doctor said it was all right for Mr. Vaslov to go to his toolshed on crutches. I helped him get settled.

"It's nice to be back here," Mr. Vaslov said.

We both looked at the table. My purple wristband was there, just where Mr. Vaslov had left it. Since he didn't know I'd taken it without asking, I figured it might be a good idea to put it back until his ankle felt better.

"So tell me," Mr. Vaslov said.

"How did the wristband work?"

I looked down at the floor. "You know I took it?"

"The wristband was on your arm when you rescued me from the roof," Mr. Vaslov said.

Mr. Vaslov sure paid attention to everything. That must be part of being a smart inventor. It was time to ask him about my new Zapato Power.

"Super bounce?" Mr. Vaslov laughed. "The wristband button makes you jump in the air?"

"You didn't give me that power on purpose?"

Mr. Vaslov shook his bushy gray head. "Lots of inventions are made by mistake."

I'd wondered about that. The purple wristband was supposed to give me controls for my super speed. Instead, it gave me super bounce!

Mr. Vaslov chuckled again. "So that's how you saw me on the roof."

I nodded my head. "I still shouldn't have taken the wristband without asking."

"True! But my new invention helped you save me."

He handed me the purple wristband. I held it in my hands,

watching the light flash in the one
clear button. With the wristband
I could control my super bounce,
but not my super speed. I handed it
back to Mr. Vaslov.

"Do you think you could add one
extra button?"

WANT MORE ZAPATO POWER?

How Freddie's adventure got started

ZAPATO POWER: FREDDIE RAMOS TAKES OFF

One day Freddie Ramos comes home from school and finds a strange box just for him. What's inside? **ZAPATO POWER**—shoes that change Freddie's life by giving him super speed!

COMING SOON!

ZAPATO POWER
FREDDIE RAMOS
ZOOMS TO THE RESCUE

Things are not going well at Starwood
Elementary! A squirrel is running
through the halls. A tree fell on the
gym. The principal is acting weird!
Can Freddie save the day with his
Zapato Power?